Splash!

A Penguin Counting Book

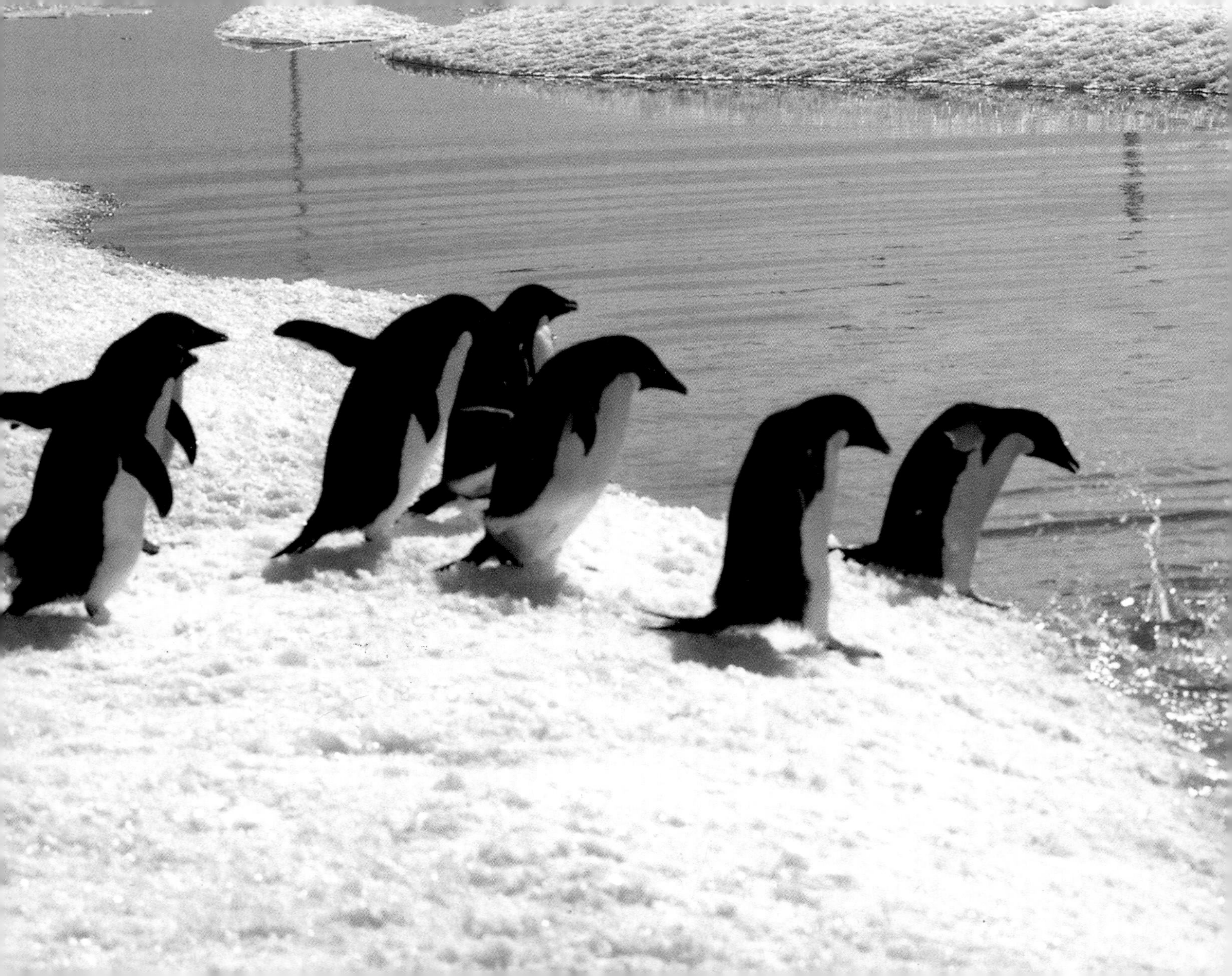

Splash!

A Penguin Counting Book

Jonathan Chester and Kirsty Melville

TRICYCLE PRESS
Berkeley, California

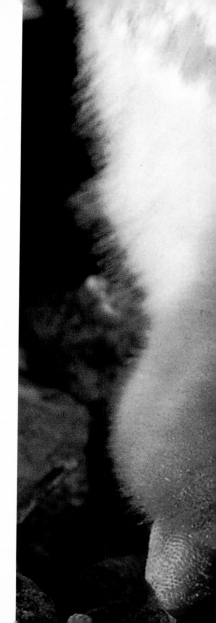

Wake up, baby penguin.

2

It's time to eat.

3

Now the chicks are all alone.

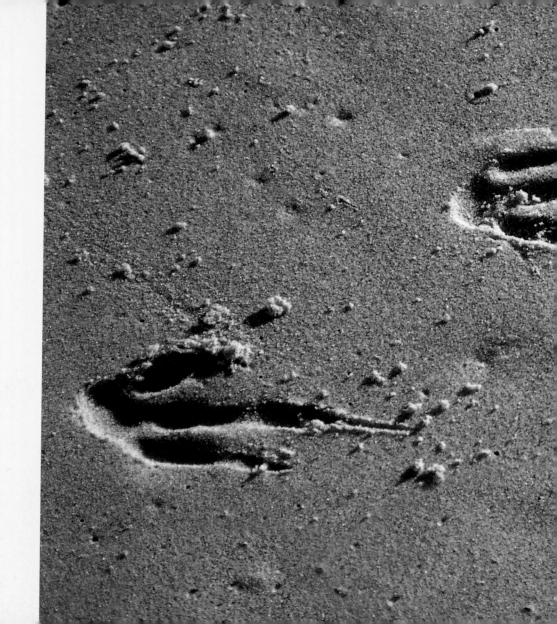

4

Where did the
grown-ups go?

5

They waddled down to...

6

...the sea!
They are going swimming
to look for food.

7

Splash!

8

Now they're full and it's time to go home. The chicks are waiting.

9

Hurry, penguins, a storm is coming!

10

Home again.
Safe at last.

Goodnight,
penguins.

How many
penguins
do you see?

Adelie penguins are flightless birds which use their feathers to keep warm. They live in large colonies on the coast of Antarctica, a continent almost entirely covered with snow and ice. A colony can have hundreds of thousands of penguins. Adult penguins leave their chicks on land while they go off to the sea in search of krill (small shrimp-like creatures). When they have swallowed enough food, they return to their colony and regurgitate the krill to feed their chicks.

Special thanks to Nicole Geiger, a talented and perceptive editor, and to Nancy Austin, an equally gifted art director.

For Debbie

 TRICYCLE PRESS
P.O. Box 7123, Berkeley, California 94707
www.tenspeed.com

Library of Congress Cataloging-in-Publication Data

Chester, Jonathan.
    Splash! : a penguin counting book / Jonathan Chester and Kirsty Melville.
        p.   cm.
    Summary: A counting book featuring photographs of Adelie penguins in their natural habitat.
    ISBN 1-883672-56-2 Casebound / ISBN 1-58246-042-6 Paperback
    1. Counting—Juvenile literature.   2. Penguins—Juvenile literature.   [1. Adelie penguin.
2. Penguins. 3. Counting.]
I. Melville, Kirsty.   II. Title.
QA113.C467   1997
513.2'11—dc21
[E]   97-8047
                                                 CIP
                                                 AC

First Tricycle Press printing, 1997
First Paperback printing, 2000
Printed in Hong Kong

1 2 3 4 5 6 — 04 03 02 01 00